PRAISE FOR

Top 10 Romance of 2012, 2015, and 2016.

— BOOKLIST: THE NIGHT IS MINE, HOT POINT,
HEART STRIKE

One of our favorite authors.

— RT BOOK REVIEWS

Buchman has catapulted his way to the top tier of my
favorite authors.

— FRESH FICTION

A favorite author of mine. I'll read anything that
carries his name, no questions asked. Meet your new
favorite author!

— THE SASSY BOOKSTER, FLASH OF FIRE

M.L. Buchman is guaranteed to get me lost in a
good story.

— THE READING CAFE, WAY OF THE WARRIOR:
NSDQ

I love Buchman's writing. His vivid descriptions bring everything to life in an unforgettable way.

HER HEART AND THE "FRIEND" COMMAND

A DELTA FORCE ROMANCE

M. L. BUCHMAN

Buchman Bookworks

SIGN UP FOR M. L. BUCHMAN'S
NEWSLETTER TODAY

and receive:
Release News
Free Short Stories
a Free Starter Library

Do it today. Do it now.
www.mlbuchman.com/newsletter

Other works by M. L. Buchman:

"*T*oday's the day, Sergey."

He watched her as she lashed on her fatigues, boots, vest, and helmet. His eyes tracked every motion as she stood over her pack in the safehouse bedroom. A grand word for a faded concrete cube, peeling whitewash, and a steel cot that might have once been comfortable, but certainly wasn't anymore. A tiny window let in the last of the day's red light and the occasional whirl of the bitter dust that southern Afghanistan used for soil.

"You'd make me feel crazy self-conscious, Sergey, if you weren't a dog." Her fifty-five pound Malinois war dog popped to his feet as she knelt beside him to strap on his own Kevlar vest. Normally he'd be kenneled rather than curled up at the foot of her bunk but, since the US military had sent her to a forward operating base in Afghanistan hell, such amenities were non-existent. She far preferred having her big furry boy asleep at her feet. They both did.

"Of course, Delta Force never is anywhere normal, are we?" She slipped the vest over his head and smoothed it down his back. Flipping the chest strap between his front legs, she buckled it into the belly of the harness. One more strap farther back and he was fully geared up. She double-checked the feed from the flip-up camera on his back and tested the infrared nightlight. Both showed up clearly on her wrist screen and her night-vision goggles. All set for a little nightwork. The small window filled with the last red of the sunset meant they'd be on the move soon.

Delta Force. We. That was such a cool sound. She'd made it. Sideways, but she'd made it into the most elite fighting force anyway. Even Delta needed MWDs—military war dogs, though she preferred multi-pawed wagging detectors—and dogs for Special Operations needed their Spec Ops handlers. Dogs for the regular forces could transfer from one handler to the next, but it took a very special person to manage a dog trained to Delta standards.

"You are so handsome in your vest, aren't you?" She rubbed his ears then brushed her hands down his legs, an automatic gesture in which she checked for everything from burrs in the fur to the condition of underlying muscle and bone.

"Where do I sign up for such treatment, Minnow?"

She sighed. Of course no world was perfect.

Elizabeth Minot—the nickname had been inevitable despite her family pronouncing it My-not—didn't bother to look up at the male voice; didn't need to turn to know what he looked like.

Garret Conway would have shoved aside the aging drape that served as the room's door with a military disregard for gender. He'd be slouching against one of the jambs, arms crossed over his chest as he glared down at the two of them with his dark brown eyes. He wasn't much taller than she was, Delta selection didn't favor tall and strong, but rather the driven and powerful. Dark hair worn long, a trim beard that eased the hard lines of his face.

So instead, she continued talking to Sergey as she finished checking him over. Pads of his paws...tail. As always, she tweaked the tip for good luck which earned her a doggie smile. All good.

"Maybe if the nasty sergeant promised to love me for a Kong dog toy and a crunchy biscuit, I'd deign to talk to him." Like she'd give the arrogant bastard the time of day. He'd been an utter twit of a boy back in the blue-collar core of Baltimore—the Dundalk neighborhood being the only thing they had in common. And just because he'd grown up into a seriously handsome soldier didn't make him any less of an SOB. She knew his dark side all too well and it was just one of the trials that the Powers That Be had placed across her path, landing her on *his* team after she'd rarely thought of him for a decade.

The fates were off at a bar crawl somewhere laughing their asses off for saddling her with him as the squad leader of her first-ever deployment with Delta. It had been a rude shock when she'd arrived this morning.

Master Sergeant Garret Conway was going to be a problem.

"Do you think he'd like a dog toy?" She asked Sergey. To make her point, Liza bounced Sergey's Kong toy on the wooden floor of the safehouse they were squatting in.

The hard rubber, shaped like a five-inch marshmallow man, ricocheted in an unexpected direction, sending Sergey pouncing, missing, and pouncing again as his attack sent it off in another direction. A frantic scuffle ensued—which included a brief strike beneath the sad excuse for a bunk—before Sergey sat back, the triumphant winner of the tussle. He smiled up at her proudly with the adoration clear in his eyes. He gave her the Kong and she traded it for a doggie treat from her pouch.

The Kong and treat were why MWDs worked so hard.

They didn't care about explosives. They just knew that when they sniffed out the explosives, they got the toy then the treat.

She fished out another treat and held it out to the squad's leader—that's how she'd think of him. Not friend—never was. Not even acquaintance from Baltimore. He'd just be Master Sergeant Conway, her Delta Force squad leader.

"Want one?" Though why she was teasing him, she didn't know.

Garret managed to take the small treat without touching her fingers. He eyed her as he bounced it in his palm. He'd been the lean and dangerous kid in high school and she could still see it in his narrowed eyes though he'd certainly filled out since then. Nobody had messed with Garret—nobody dared. He'd always had a circle of wannabes, but he hadn't needed them. It was more as if he was a one-man center of dark power and the others had merely been drawn like night moths. No matter where she went in the school, it had always seemed that he was there in the background watching. He missed nothing.

Occasionally, if she'd wanted to track someone down, she'd ask him. That was about the only time they ever spoke, but he always knew. She knew almost nothing about him. His dad was a stevedore down at the port—the kind who drank too much when he got home. Her dad was a machinist who didn't. It bothered her that she couldn't remember more about him.

Garret had always had a hot girl under his arm at every school dance or block party. He'd never been picky on the last count: athlete, cheerleader, from another school (a big social crime that only he could get away with), slut… Never mattered as long as she was built. Liza once again blessed her lean figure that had served her so well in track and field, and in the Army. Surviving her three brothers had developed her strength early and she'd never let that advantage go.

When her dad had slipped a German Shepard pup under the tree for her fifth Christmas, she'd found her calling. The two of them had played and run together until a car had killed him when she was seventeen. By then he was slow, mostly deaf, and blind in one eye.

She'd been walking him home from the vet who had given the worst pronouncement of all—cancer, with only days to live. She often wondered if Rex had known what he was doing when he'd stepped off the curb before she released him. It had been instantaneous, merciful, and utterly horrifying. When she'd looked up from Rex's suddenly lax form into Garret Conway's eyes, she didn't know whether to thank him or try to kill him.

Liza still didn't.

Garret continued to watch her as he fooled with the treat. Then—with no more words than he'd offered on that horrible day while he'd put Rex in her lap in the back seat and driven her back to the vet to arrange for cremation—he held the treat out for Sergey.

Sergey's sharp snarl had him jerking his hand back.

"What the hell?"

"I haven't told him that you're a friend. He's very careful."

"So tell him, Minnow." Half the high school had gone to "Little Fish." At least he'd never done that.

Tell Sergey that Garret was a friend? Not in a thousand years. But the dog only knew the one word. She had no way to explain "asshole from my past but don't attack him" to a dog. There was *friend* and there was *attack*.

Finally, she simply said, "Down."

Sergey lay down immediately, but continued glaring at Garret. *Good dog.*

2

---

*G*arret didn't know which of the two looked more dangerous: the tall slip of a blonde or her damn dog. It was clear that neither was glad to see him.

Of all the possible soldiers command could have sent his way, why did it have to be her? Had someone seen the shared high school in their past and decided they were doing him a favor? No. They'd looked at skills and decided she was the best fit for the job based on skills and availability—meaning she'd already been in the dustbowl rather than having to be shipped in from the States.

He didn't doubt that for a second. She'd always been one of those overachiever types. A top student and the school's star decathlete. After watching her win seven-of-ten events in a decathlon, easily winning the overall event freshman year, he'd tried out for the team. That's when he'd discovered what an amazing athlete she truly was. The coach had kicked him loose after three events: not the first cut, but almost. Thank god she hadn't been around that day to see his humiliation.

The next year, he'd made it through all of the events

before being cut. He'd finally made the team the year she went All-State—the football team. He was fast and knew how to take a hit—but it wasn't enough to shine among the guys who'd caught their first pass as they were leaving the womb. He'd graduated second string and hadn't liked it.

Minnow was the gold standard of women. It sucked that he'd never been able to speak to her. The beautiful, popular, star athlete shone with a brightness that made his life feel even darker and dirtier than it was.

He tossed the dog treat down in front of the Malinois. Sergey didn't even track it to the floor—his attention remained riveted on Garret's face, and not in a good way. His muscles remained bunched and ready for action.

"We've got some chow in the other room," he said to Minnow. "Briefing in ten. Out the door in twenty." Then he turned his back on them and walked back to join the rest of the team.

"It's okay," he heard her speak softly to the dog.

There was a sharp snap of jaws that took all of Garret's training not to react to. Then he heard the quick crunch as Sergey ate the treat he must have snapped up.

The hut's other room was just as disgusting as the sole bedroom he'd given Minnow and her dog. Their safehouse was little more than the smallest of three huts inside a massive ring of HESCO barriers and piles of sandbags. A dozen years of occupancy by a rotating stream of NATO forces hadn't been kind to it. A small firepit, a table covered in his team's gear, wooden pegs driven into cracks in the concrete from which their rifles dangled on their straps. Regular forces were standing security outside, so at least they didn't have to think about that. The other four Unit operators were too quiet and had clearly heard everything.

"Mutt and Jeff," Maxwell and Jaffe, the nickname inevitable as they were two jokers like a comedy routine, ping-ponging remarks back and forth. They could go all day if he let them. One tall and at least a little thoughtful, the other short and quick-witted. They were also both crack shots.

"Both of you load up long."

No need to tell them twice. They opened hard-shell cases and began assembling their preferred sniper rifles. Predictably Mutt favored an old-school Accuracy International AWM and Jeff ran with a hot-rod Remington M2010 that he'd hand-modified—only a true sniper tinkered with a ten thousand dollar rifle. Both were barreled for the .300 Win Mag cartridges, so that they could swap ammo if needed.

"BB," Burton and Baxter on the other hand, could be addressed interchangeably. As different and distinct as Mutt and Jeff were, the BB boys weren't. Both explosive and electronic techs, they were generally quiet but had a habit of finishing each other's sentences. No sign of a sense of humor, it was just something they did. One from Oregon, the other from Idaho and despite three years together he wasn't sure which one. They'd both kicked their pasts to the curb, which sounded good to him—as if he couldn't feel the past and her dog watching him through the doorway at his back.

It still felt strange to be in charge of the team. Chris had just recently opted out after his wife Azadah came down with an incurable condition, becoming mother of his first child. Since when did hard-core Delta operators turn all mushy? The answer: since he'd fallen in love with an Afghan refugee during the team's three-month deployment in Lashkar Gah and taken her home. Just because she'd helped them take down some of the top "most wanted" in southern Afghanistan was no reason to fall in love with her. At least not that he could see.

What had been crazy was that none of them had noticed

her while she'd been working as their cook and charwoman —except Chris. Yet when Garret had seen her at the wedding in upstate New York, she was so stunning it was hard to believe. High-born, fallen on hard times during all of the wars, fluent in several languages (including a soft English), she had somehow shifted from being invisible to being impossible to look away from. The woman had glowed and Chris, the lucky asshole, had never looked so happy in the six years he and Garret had served together.

But Garret wasn't going to have any of that. He'd finally found himself in The Unit, as Delta called them themselves. No way was he leaving except if they carried him out and *that* was something no operator really thought about.

It felt even stranger being in charge with Liza aboard. He couldn't imagine that Minnow would be any less than an amazing asset—he just wasn't sure how he was going to survive it.

3

---

*T*here hadn't been time to really meet the others when she'd slipped into Wesh, Afghanistan along with the pre-dawn light. The Unit had been returning from a long patrol and had crashed into their bedrolls. Even less talkative than normal for Unit operators; which was saying something. They'd obviously been pushing hard.

Unsure what to do or how to behave—and totally unnerved at finding Garret Conway in command—Liza had taken his gesture toward the back room as banishment and hunkered down. In the middle of the night she'd decided that there was no way he'd get the best of her and ruin her first chance with The Unit.

So, she entered the main room as confidently as she could.

Sergey was her envoy. She kept him on a tight lead, which was completely for show as she could command him much more accurately and quickly with gestures and voice commands.

She greeted each one the same way, "If you'd hold out your hand for Sergey to get your scent." As each one did, she'd clearly say, "Friend." Each time Sergey would look up at her to make sure, then take a sniff and accept a pat on the head.

"Don't know what your problem is, Conway," tall-and-lean Mutt tickled Sergey's ears. "Looks like a sweetheart to me."

"Just a big old mushball, aren't you?" Jeff, Mutt's short-and-solid sidekick, gave her dog a neck rub.

"I don't know…" Baxter was more interested in checking out the vest with light and camera than the animal wearing it.

"…looks ready for a Spec Ops mission to me," Burton finished. Both were middle-build and Nordic blond. It would be hard not to get them mixed up except that Burton paid some attention to Sergey before checking out the dog's military vest himself. He looked to Sergey rather than her for permission before he reached out to toy with the camera—a gesture Liza appreciated.

The infrared and daylight camera was center-mounted on his back with a flip mount so that it could fold forward or back in case Sergey needed to squeeze in or out of a small space. It also had an infrared light to really illuminate the darkness when needed. A Lexan faceplate protected the lens. The antenna mounted close beside it was a flexible whip rather than a knockdown.

Then they both inspected the feed to the screen on Liza's wrist.

"Very cool!" Baxter noted.

"Thanks!" Burton rubbed Sergey's head in appreciation for his patience.

She had the feeling that she was invisible to the men, as she often did when Sergey was beside her. No complaints from her. Let them focus on the dog, she didn't need their praise, only his.

Then she turned to Garret...no, Conway. Everyone else called him Conway and so would she. Once more he slouched against a wall, sporking his way through an MRE—Meal-Ready-to-Eat—straight out of the bag. Shredded BBQ Beef, with black beans and notoriously soggy tortillas, for breakfast.

She stopped Sergey two steps from Conway. Sergey didn't strain on the leash, but she could feel his tension vibrating up its length. Or maybe her tension vibrating down it.

The dog always knows what the trainer feels, she repeated her trainer's prime axiom. *Always. So only feel what you want the dog to feel.*

Liza took a deep breath to calm herself.

"Friend," she managed. Though it was harder than she'd expected—and she hadn't thought it would be easy.

Sergey and Conway both looked at her in surprise. Here was one man who saw her clearly behind the dog. He lowered his hand for Sergey to smell, but didn't look away from her.

She could feel her dog still looking at her in question.

"It's okay," she repeated, though she wasn't sure for whose benefit.

4

---

*L*ast night's patrol—and the five nights before that—had narrowed down their mission. Narrowed it down enough for Garret to know they'd need all the help they could get, specifically from a MWD. He'd sent the request up the chain of command and they'd sent back down Sergey and Minnow.

Time to just live with it. Just this one assignment, then she'd be gone back into the vast world of US Army Human Resources Command and wash up on someone else's shore. That knowledge, like so much in the military, was both a relief and a knife to the gut.

He unrolled the map of Wesh, Afghanistan, and the near edge of Chaman, Pakistan, separated by the towering, dual-arched Friendship Gate.

"The Durand Line, the border between Afghanistan and Pakistan, is over two thousand kilometers long from Iran up to India. It is generally named as the most dangerous border in the world—which if you've done time in Korea you know is saying something. The two countries have been fighting over it ever since the line was first drawn in 1893 by the

Brits and the Afghan Amir. Oddly, Pakistan is fine with the line, it's the Afghanis who say they'll never accept the border."

"Whoever would want this stretch of desert is welcome to it."

"Pashtuns, dude." Mutt and Jeff were at it again. "The Pashtun tribes cover thousands of square kilometers on both sides."

"Then why are they killing each other if they're all Pashtuns?"

"Not our business," Garret cut them off. Because there were a hundred layers of answers to that question: some historical, some religious, some about power, and none of it good for the locals.

He could feel Minnow assessing their group dynamics. It made him see himself and all his flaws as a commander as if seeing himself through stranger's eyes. Too rough? Or just holding the team's focus? He couldn't think how to change the patterns even if he understood what they were. Chris had always made it look so easy. How was he supposed to know that leadership was such a pain in the ass.

"Our business is that Wesh-Chaman is the only crossing for hundreds of kilometers in both directions. All through the Afghan War—"

"Which one?"

And again it spun out of his control before he even—

"The one that started with Alexander the Great. That was like three hundred AD or something."

"Three-thirty BC, dude, learn your history. And no, he's talking about the one that started in 1978 with the Communist Insurrection and hasn't stopped since. Next came the Soviets, the communist collapse, the Taliban, and then us. No wonder this place is a disaster area. Did you know—"

"Shut up, Jeff," Garret shut them down harder this time.

"I'm talking about the US War in Afghanistan and you assholes know it so give me a goddamn break. This Wesh-Chaman crossing has been our major supply route since Day One for all of southern Afghanistan. Still is, since we haven't really left, and it's coming apart, again. Tonight we're going to put some of it back together, again."

"Good. I was getting bored. How about you, Sergey?" Mutt rubbed the dog's neck where he lay between Mutt and Liza. Sergey just scowled up at him, Garret-radar on red alert. The dog wasn't having anything to do with the "friend" instruction no matter what Minnow commanded.

Garret continued. "They sent in a reinforced platoon of over sixty regular Army, and they found squat. Now it's Delta's turn."

The five of them, a woman, and her dog.

"The US has had constant problems with the Paki gunrunners supplying the Afghanis. In turn, the Pakis have been getting nailed by the Afghani militants who think shelling civilians across the border during a census-taking makes some kind of sense. Just last week they blew up another pair of fuel tanker semi-trucks. Not like the sixteen they got at once back in 2009, but—"

"Can you imagine what..." Baxter joined in for the first time.

"...two hundred thousand gallons was like..." Burton was on it.

"...all at once?" Baxter sighed for having missed such a spectacle.

"Ka-boom!" they said together and both sighed again. They were both explosives techs, so he let them have their moment.

"I'm lead," Garret told them. "BB, you're both hot on my tail. Mutt and Jeff, you alternate sniper overwatch and watching the back doors."

"Where do you want us?" Liza had her hand dug into the dog's fur. He could see that her knuckles were white no matter how calm her voice was.

"You, Minnow, are glued to my hip."

And wasn't that going to be fun.

5

The buildings of Wesh were pitch black—invisible except as dark notches out of the stars. Without her night-vision goggles she couldn't have made it ten steps. No street lights and what electricity the town did have was apparently on the fritz per usual in small Afghan towns. A few windows were lit by the flickering of oil lamps, a very few. It was a town with air conditioning, and one that needed it desperately. She and Sergey had been tramping through Afghan hell for three months now and neither of them were any more used to the heat than the day they landed.

"What are we after?" Liza eased down the narrow street far closer to Garret Conway than she'd ever been to him in high school. Much to her surprise, she'd liked watching him with the men. Whatever else she might think of him, his men trusted him completely. This wasn't some cluster of syco-phantic hallway teens; these were top Unit operators.

"Sergey's specialty," Garret kept his voice low. "There is a constant stream of explosives moving in both directions here. Bombs for inbound NATO supply trucks headed into Kandahar and Lashkar Gah. And Taliban and other pissed-off Afghanis going into Pakistan to blow the crap out of shrines and the civilian populace. I don't care which side is holding it, I just want it gone. No matter which way it's headed, it comes through Wesh. We want the bombmakers and their middlemen."

Wesh was laid out differently than most Afghan towns she'd patrolled. Usually they were a rabbit warren of streets which had evolved for donkeys and pedestrians. But the old Silk Road had passed through here since the Romans began trading with the Chinese and probably before that. The town was sliced by the one wide main street that must date back thousands of years. Rather than being lined with haphazard two-story structures that were connected only by the chance of shared walls, the main road was lined to either side with long rows of stone one-story warehouses. Each warehouse was a great V with dozens of storefronts and storage bays facing inward—the open end of the V facing the trade road. They served the only passage between the countries for a long way around.

At the head of the first V, Garret stopped at the corner of the building where they were in deepest shadow.

BB were close behind them.

Jeff had peeled off to go down the back side of the building in case they flushed anyone out that way.

Conway tapped her shoulder then pointed across the street and up. With her night-vision goggles, she could just make out Mutt on top of the only two-story building for several hundred meters around. He then indicated for her to lead the way, pointing close along the line of closed shops.

She turned on the feed from Sergey's camera in one eye of her NVGs. For brightness, she selected a level that didn't distract her, but she could see as an overlay if she concentrated on it. Originally, it had been a vertiginous experience —disorienting dog-style motion fed into the human eye—but she'd learned to use and finally appreciate it. Wherever Sergey went, she could feel the connection between them until they functioned as one.

She knelt next to Sergey, gave him a good scratch, then whispered, "Seek." A hand gesture—that she knew he could see even if it was too dark for unaided human eyes—was all the direction he needed.

In that instant, he transformed. He would no longer react well to anyone trying to touch him, but neither would he be bothered by Garret Conway standing a foot away. He now had only one task in mind—sniffing out one of the thousand-plus explosives compounds he'd been trained to recognize.

Trusting her, he stepped around the corner and began working his way along the line of shops. She swung loose her FN-SCAR assault rifle, double-checked that the flash suppressor was in place and moved in behind him. Sergey trailed his nose along the base of battered wood and steel garage doors that shuttered each bay of the long building.

Fifty meters down, he skipped a narrow doorway, probably leading up a set a stairs to the roof. She snapped her fingers lightly, calling him back. He double-checked where she indicated, but showed no interest, so she waved him to continue.

After the third building with no "alert," she could feel the team's growing impatience.

But she knew she couldn't share that. Couldn't let Sergey know or he'd pick up on it, get distracted or hurry at the wrong moment.

She signaled him along the fourth building and followed in his footsteps.

6

*G*arret didn't know whether to be thrilled or worried. If his team had been searching on their own, they'd still be back at the first building, breaking into bay after bay of worthless garbage. Some of it would be household belongings, stored when refugees had been told they couldn't take them across the border—all held in the hopes of returning someday. Foodstuffs, manufacturing supplies, bicycle parts, the list was endless. The locks were feeble at best, easily picked. But each lock took time. Each inspection was visual and usually tedious.

But the dog went by each bay as fast as they could walk.

This was either fast…or useless. What if they'd walked by some major weapons cache?

He'd worked with military war dogs before, but always as point on a patrol, sniffing out buried IEDs. He'd never let a MWD guide the destination of an entire mission.

As they moved to the fifth warehouse, he couldn't help watching Minnow. She moved like her nickname: quick, smooth, hardly disturbing the air around her. In a land where standing still and just breathing could produce a rising cloud of brownout dust, she and her dog barely stirred the air as they slipped along.

Get her out of your head, Conway! Being distracted by anything on a mission was bad news. He thought that had been trained out of him, but apparently not.

Liza could distract a dead man already in his grave. That pleasant, can-do attitude she'd struck with the team this evening had been pitch perfect. She'd won all four guys over with her polite introduction and her ever-so-gentle but obviously dangerous-as-hell companion. He pitied the man who tried to touch her uninvited.

Minnow had also stood out because of how she looked. They'd all been in-country for a week and looked it. She'd arrived from wherever she'd been, looking fresh-showered and poster perfect. Her straight blonde hair swinging just along her fine jaw line. Her blue eyes wide and observant. Her smile easy—for everyone except him. And the way she acted with the dog was just too much.

Like the one that he'd murdered and never been able to apologize for, it was clear that she loved her dog and that the feeling was returned. Together they—

Sergey sat abruptly and Garret almost plowed into Minnow when she stopped as well.

The dog was looking up at her expectantly, his tongue lolling happily.

"What?" He was so close to here that he barely had to whisper. As close as lovers.

Shit! He'd just been in the field too long. Had to be to think such things.

Minnow made the throat-cutting signal with her hand meaning danger, then pointed emphatically at the closed door.

Oh! Pay dirt. Sitting was the dog's signal of a find.

She quickly guided Sergey forward, pointing at the ground. He sniffed the ground, but kept walking. No IEDs. Then she led him to the opposite edge of the door. Once more he sat abruptly.

Garret clicked his mic and whispered, "West side, bay seven."

Jeff was now on sniper overwatch and Mutt was on the ground out back. Mutt would position himself to deal with anyone trying to escape that way.

Burton came forward to pick the lock, but hesitated at the door. He swung his hand forward, the sign for point of entry. Then he made an non-standard gesture like twisting a door-knob. Like—

There was no lock for him to unlock. Garret checked the door edges again. No light leakage. It was a double, wooden door, with handles and a wear line where a chain and padlock had hung. The doors would swing out to either side.

In case it was booby-trapped, or a gunman waited in the dark, Garret yanked out a length of tactical line and tied it to one handle. Burton did the same to the other door. He had them switch sides, which confused Burton, but that was just tough. They each backed up holding the end of the line. Burton stood beside Baxter and, as he'd planned, Garret ended up between Minnow and the dog.

He held up three fingers…two…braced himself, then yanked open the doors.

A heavy sheet of black plastic hung just inside the doors, blocking all light.

"Tsook?" a voice asked "Who?" through the black plastic.

Garret held up a fist to freeze the team in place.

Someone pulled aside one edge of the plastic less than two feet from where Garret stood with his back against the now open door. The man was backlit by a kerosene or oil lamp and would be night blind. Like most Afghan men, he was thin, weather-beaten, and wore a thin black beard.

"*Tsook?*" he asked again.

Garret reached out, grabbed him by the throat, and dragged him out through the plastic. As the material flapped aside, he didn't see anyone else inside. He thumped the man in the solar plexus hard enough to make sure he wouldn't be crying out an alarm in the next few moments, then passed him back to the soldier behind him.

That would be Minnow! *Crap!* No choice. He handed the man off and hoped for the best.

He used his rifle barrel to brush aside the plastic as Baxter did the same on the other side. Two women squatted low over an entire array of armament. There were dozens of AK-47s and several rocket-propelled grenades. An old Toyota Land Cruiser SUV was stripped down, ready to be turned into a rolling bomb. Everything would be hidden inside door panels, fenders, and seats. The only thing they lacked was a pile of something that exploded to shove inside the exposed cavities.

In moments, Minnow had handed off her prisoner and had the two women bound. Dealing with another woman, the two Afghani women were surprised, but calm. If a man had done it, they'd fight and scream because no married woman was supposed to be touched by another man. Minnow hadn't missed a single trick. No matter how fresh she looked, she'd clearly spent plenty of time in-country.

He squatted down and began questioning the man, who just kept shaking his head in refusal.

That's when he noticed Minnow. She had Sergey playing his nice-doggie game. Garret never heard the word "friend" but neither was the Malinois poised to rend.

Unable to get anything from the man, he finally gagged him just as Minnow signaled Garret to the other corner.

BB made fast work of completely securing the area and clearing the weapons.

"Couldn't get shit out of him," Garret grumbled.

"The women are waiting," Minnow replied. "They aren't happy about it either, but he's brother to one and husband to the other so they have little choice."

"For what?"

"There's a shipment coming tonight," she waved toward the partially disassembled car. "A big load of explosives. Coming here. Not for a while, but it's coming."

Now *that* was good news.

He stopped BB before they could burn some thermite and melt the weapons cache. Everything had to look normal. He deployed his team as well as he could, restoring the black-out plastic, closing the doors, as well as arranging a few other surprises. He roamed the room. All the tools of a car mechanic's shop were piled along one wall, but no spare parts—new or used. The man was a car-bomb producer. Pull in a car, receive a delivery of explosives and, presto chango, mass destruction in a marketplace.

The front had been cleared for the pending delivery. A stripped Land Cruiser SUV stood in the middle of the bay. The guy was good. He'd welded steel struts in place of the springs. It would make for a hard ride, but the suspension wouldn't sag—a common indicator of a car loaded down heavy with explosives. Near one back corner, past the stack of dismounted fenders and seats, stood the refuse pile—all the stripped-out metal, springs, fittings, even spare tires from prior car-bomb conversions. There was a small gap along the back wall for access to the rear door. He made sure it was secure. To the other side stood a massive, rusted-out truck's engine block. He stashed his prisoners behind that.

At the center of the back wall he was able to sit with a view of the whole bay. He dropped into place with his back against the wall to do what Delta did best—be patient and wait.

A low growl informed him that he should have landed somewhere other than close beside Minnow and her furry guardian.

7

"*S*hush!"

Sergey huffed grumpily then lay his head on her thigh, effectively pinning her in place. That blocked any excuse for getting away from Conway.

"How long until the shipment arrives?" Conway checked his watch for the twentieth time in the last ten minutes.

"I still don't know."

"Right. Sorry."

They sat in silence long enough for Sergey to finally relax with a sigh.

"Doesn't like me much."

"You never gave *me* a reason to," which Liza decided was just the truth. She never had, though she was definitely learning to respect the man he'd grown into.

"Murdering your dog. Guess not." Liza could hear the hard knot of pain and self-recrimination in Conway's voice.

"He was dead already."

Conway glared at the ceiling. He'd rested his HK416 rifle butt down between his legs and draped his hands over the protrusion of the foregrip handle. "You saying that you tossed a dead dog in front of my car for the fun of it? I saw him walking."

Liza could feel that awful day coming back over her. Rex had slowed down the few days prior. He'd been old, but still enjoying his play and his food, then suddenly he didn't anymore. It had been everything she could do to not weep after the diagnosis as she walked him home. "One last walk to say goodbye." They'd spend one last night together in her bed then she'd have to put him down in the morning. And then…

"He was a dead dog walking," her voice sounded like a croaking frog, but she held it together. She certainly wasn't going to lose it in front of Garret Conway of all people. Or on a mission. She distracted herself by telling him about the blindness, deafness, and finally cancer. And not just a little, but riddling his body. "Sometimes I think he stepped in front of your car on purpose, just to spare me having to hold his paw while they injected him."

Now Garret was looking down at her, "He was sick? I didn't know."

She could only nod and look down at her hand buried deep in Sergey's fur.

After a long silence—that she couldn't look up from—she could feel him turn to study the ceiling once more. "Well, ain't that some news. You never said."

"The shock, Garret. It was so big. You hit him less than five minutes after I staggered out of the vet's office. I wasn't ready to lose him. Not slowly, not fast. Dad gave him to me when I was five. I have almost no memories prior to him. Then he was gone. It was a blessing in disguise. But I sure wasn't ready to talk about it that day. And afterwards…" all she could do was shrug. "We never spoke much in school."

She heard a soft *thump*, then another, and looked up to see him banging the back of his head against the stone wall.

"What?"

"You and that dog changed my life."

"No we didn't." It was a ridiculous idea.

Then he looked over at her. The deep brown of his eyes so close that she couldn't look away. They'd been almost shoulder-to-shoulder, and now they were nearly nose-to-nose.

"Trust me," his voice went soft and low. "You and he absolutely did."

8

*A*nd Garret couldn't believe he'd just confessed such a thing. *Keep it professional.* Yeah, too late for that. He was a Unit operator, not a throwback, useless-shit of a self-absorbed testosterone-laden... But he still couldn't believe he'd told her.

And the apology that he'd rehearsed a thousand times in his head, but never found a way to say through the rest of senior year, he couldn't manage now either.

He wanted to look away, he *needed* to look away. But there she was, looking at him with those wide blue eyes the color of a summer sky and he couldn't move. He'd often hung out at the piers along the Patapsco River, waiting for his dad and watching that sky. She was like the only good part of home.

"How did *my* dog change *your* life?"

"Not just your dog."

Sergey looked up suddenly, inspecting her rather than him. Then Garret noticed her white-knuckled hand buried in his ruff.

"Um, you may want to ease up on your dog there."

At that, she finally looked away and he felt as if he'd been released from some sort of hypnosis ray. She eased her death grip and apologized to the dog. Sergey inspected him with curiosity, but no longer animosity.

Then Minnow looked back up at him and he was trapped again by the eyes that were windows right down into her.

"How is it you're still single, Minnow?" Not a question he had ever thought he'd be asking.

She shrugged. "Why?"

"You—" he stumbled to a halt. "I—" *really need to shut the hell up.* "You—" he tried again. "Shit!" he gave up trying and went back to beating his head against the stone wall. Why couldn't the terrorist bastards just show up already? He'd take 'em down. Maybe get a lead on some arms supplier. Interrupt and destroy a big weapons delivery. He knew how to do those. How to talk to Liza Minot was obviously beyond him.

"Garret, you can't just say something like that and not explain it. How did my poor old dog change *your* life?"

Well, at least she was back to that topic. He had some chance of explaining that without screwing up.

"Because I could never run like you." Or perhaps he couldn't help screwing up around her. Giving up, he explained himself.

9

*L*iza could only watch Garret with amazement.

He explained his failed attempts to make the track-and-field team to get her attention. *Her* attention. She was a nobody, just a better than average student who had learned how to run and throw so that she could keep up with her older brothers. She been outfielder at home softball games by seven and pitcher by nine. Though after several "slobber ball" complaints, she'd had to teach Rex that if he wanted to sit on the mound with her, he wasn't allowed to chase softballs. Tennis balls, of course, were fair game. He was a major disruption when neighborhood games of stick ball had spilled out onto the hot summer streets.

"Your dog…"

Liza finally realized that Garret didn't even know Rex's name, so she told him.

"Thanks. Killing Rex made me give up on you. No way you were ever going to talk to the guy who murdered your dog."

"But it wasn't—"

"So you tell me now. I'm still not so sure. Anyway. I knew

what I had to do. Even just to live with myself, I was going to have to get truly good at something."

"And you chose the toughest team in the entire military."

He nodded, "And I chose the toughest team in the entire military. Made it too."

She could hear the pride in his voice. Except he was a guy, so it was more like self-satisfaction. Now that he'd made it, *of course* he'd made it. As if any past doubts (and past failings) had been erased by his actual success.

And maybe they had.

"You're not the Garret Conway I knew in school."

"I'm hoping that's a good thing."

She didn't know how to answer, because she wasn't sure what the question was any more. He'd held some kind of a ludicrous torch for her, which had driven him into Delta. Yet, at the same time, he'd given up that torch, and thrown himself completely into becoming a truly superior soldier.

Somehow she and Rex had changed a man's life. And knowing that brought back all the grief she had shut down so hard all those years ago. She missed Rex all over again like a hole in her heart. Yet his final act had been to change a man's life for the better. And again she wondered if it had been conscious. Or some weird doggie sense of what was needed? It would be just too unlikely if it was merely coincidence.

Her head was whirling and she wondered if she was going to lose the Maple Pork Sausage Patty with Pepper and Onions MRE that had been her breakfast hours ago.

"I'm going to go and check on things," Garret leveraged himself to his feet. But before he stepped away, he rested his hand on her shoulder for just a moment. "It's good to see you, Minnow." Then he was across the room checking nothing in particular that she could see.

10

They came at moonset. The darkest part of the Afghan night.

Mutt and Jeff had a brief debate over which of them heard the vehicles first. The trucks were coming from the Afghanistan side, so the targets must be the Pakis—this time. Did this bombmaker service both sides? Probably not. He struck Garret as more the fanatic type.

Three Toyota pickups. Most of the traffic to the Friendship Gate was by foot, bicycle, and burro-drawn carts. The motorized traffic was almost entirely massive trucks. There were the NATO and US supply trucks carrying exactly the labeled load limit. These were accompanied by heavily armed patrols to deter anyone attaching an explosive charge to them. The other trucks were just as big, but loaded ludicrously beyond anything the rigs had ever been designed for. Loose hay, bags of grain or rice, stacks upon stacks of bricks, anything—all piled so high that it was a miracle the trucks didn't tip over every time they hit a pothole. These were driven with reckless abandon and had been a staple of the region since forever.

Small Toyotas were good utility trucks, but they were fantastic field vehicles for roving military. Tough, reliable, four-wheel drive, and able to carry a heavy load. Not armored, but cheap and plentiful.

Mutt and Jeff were both on rooftops now. They reported that two of the three were loaded to past the limits beneath heavy tarps. It was the middle vehicle that was worrisome. Someone had mounted a DShK Russian heavy machine gun on its bed. Its round could punch through an inch of armor. If that's what they had in the open, it meant the men in the cabs would have plenty of automatic weapons.

He yanked the Afghani to his feet and pulled his gag.

"You will say the code words, and you will say them properly."

When the man started to protest, Garret yanked his sidearm and rammed the barrel up under the man's jaw.

"Pohidal?"

He decided to take the man's wide eyes as a yes that he "understood."

Until Minnow called out to him, "The woman said that her husband is very stubborn."

"Shit!" He didn't have time for this. Garret swung his sidearm aside, then smashed it back against the man's temple. He dropped like a brick.

Minnow helped him drag the man back into a safe spot where the other two women were tied behind the truck engine block.

BB were front and back on the roof of this long arm of the warehouse's V-shape, ready to fire from above or drop down if needed.

His snipers were on opposing rooftops for maximum coverage—one across the main street, the other looking down from the next block back.

That left him, Minnow, and her dog in the equipment bay

itself. Bad planning, but his need to keep her close had gotten them here and it was too late to change their plan. Especially as his goal was to keep some of the bad guys alive long enough to get more information about the supply chain.

He crossed to where she was watching the back door from the same protected corner that held their three hostages.

"You keep low and you stay alive, hear?"

She nodded then, after a long pause, "You, too."

No time to think about what that pause might mean.

---

*L*iza was thinking about that pause and wondering where it had come from. It was more than something she'd wish for a fellow soldier. She wanted Garret to…what?

Garret—funny how Conway just wouldn't stick anymore —made it a half dozen paces away before he stopped as if he'd been shot. He spun to face her before rushing back. For half a moment she thought he might be coming to kiss her. What reaction that might call for died before it had a chance to be considered as he brushed by her.

"Help me get this guy stripped!" He whipped out a knife and sliced the Afghani's bonds.

"Get undressed," she told him, because she knew what he was after. She took over removing the unconscious man's clothes. Garret was far more powerfully built, but clothes here were loose to fend off the heat. She had all of the man's clothes off and had re-lashed his wrists in case he woke, before turning to offer the clothes to Garret.

Down to his socks and boxers, he was *very much* not the boy she remembered. Muscle rippled over him with every gesture. His job hadn't left him untouched. A long knife scar across his ribs. A bullet wound through one thigh. A spattering of scars that could only come from being caught by a cloud of shrapnel. None of that showed on his face or hands, but his body could only belong to a warrior.

Garret dressed quickly and she did her best not to blush as she helped him, pulling up his *partug* (the blousy pants) and leaving him to figure out how to tie it tightly across his flat stomach while she re-laced his boots. The *khet* over his head, then she was buttoning the cuffs while he tried to settle the draping shirt so that it fell cleanly to his knees.

They kept bumping together in awkward and surprising ways. He couldn't wear his military vest, but the Afghani's vest of brown linen fell past his hips and she was soon ducked under the edge of it to lash Garret's knife's scabbard around one thigh, reaching between his legs to do the lacing.

"A hundred meters," she echoed Mutt's report for him because he'd had to shed his radio to get the pillbox *kufi* hat to sit properly on his head.

She worked her way up his body, tucking sidearms, spare magazines, and grenades where she could. With each oddly intimate contact she became more and more aware of him. When she finished straightening his collar, he'd made a mess of it, it left her hands holding the narrow collar close about his throat.

Liza leaned in and kissed him for luck. Kissed him for welcoming her in and not holding their past against her. To thank him for giving Rex a merciful death. And to thank him for the man he'd become.

Before he could really respond, she pulled back.

"Fifty meters," she took away his HK416 that instinct had returned to his hands and stuffed an AK-47 into them.

Then she turned him to face the front door.

"Go!" She slapped him on the ass to send him on his way,

then she hunkered down in her hiding spot beside Sergey and tried not to laugh at her presumption and his surprise.

"Ready," she whispered to her dog. In moments he was standing and in full alert mode. Nothing would be catching them by surprise.

There were two piles of junk in the back of the long warehouse bay. She shooed Sergey over behind one pile, while she crouched in front of the unconscious man and the two bound women.

Before she could take another breath, Garret had stuck his head out through the black plastic and called out into the night, *"Tsook?"*

arret felt he did a passable job of explaining that his "good friend" was home sick and had sent him in the man's place.

"Yes, poor Hukam," the man's wife was suddenly beside him.

Even with things happening so fast, Minnow had remembered that the woman was unhappy about the explosives delivery. And now here she was helping him.

"Something he ate," she continued. "It must have come from Pakistan."

In covering his surprise, he glanced away…and spotted his own HK416 in Liza's hands where she peeked around the engine block. It was aimed at the back of the woman's head and Hukam's wife must know it. Okay, maybe she had a couple of reasons to be so cooperative.

Garret turned back and wondered how long the ruse might hold up. Not very long.

"Come. We must hurry. Unload so that you may begin the long drive back. I hope the journey was not too hard."

The leader kept his weapon on Garret, but seemed to

agree with the urgency. "You stand aside. We will unload."
And he waved the first pickup to back in.

Garret moved to the side wall and was pleased to see that
Liza was out of sight, except for a dog tail. Thankfully Sergey
wasn't wagging it, but rather standing stock still. Hopefully
no one would notice.

Impossible to still think of her as Minnow after that kiss.
If she'd wanted him more alert than he'd ever been in his life,
she'd figured out how to get him there. Every nuance of that
kiss was implanted on his nervous system which was now
running at the full-adrenaline setting. He didn't have time to
wonder if there was more to that kiss than making sure he
was on point, but it had sure as hell worked.

"See?" He tried to distract the leader—and ignore the AK-
47 pointed at his gut. "See? We have the car ready." A glance
revealed that the incoming supplies were mostly C-4. This
was no diesel fuel and fertilizer operation. A lot of money
had gone into this effort and they'd stumbled on it because of
Liza and her dog.

And the quantity! This many close-packed bricks of C-4
could take down a Parliament building or a Presidential
Palace.

A part of him babbled on as if he was extremely proud of
his work. Another wished he knew what the hell his team
was doing—the lack of radio contact was making him crazy.

Garret tried to keep between the leader and the exposed
length of Sergey's tail while the second truck was being
unloaded.

*I*f Garret didn't move soon, Liza was going to shoot him.

She squatted behind the engine block with the prisoners, which gave her one good line of sight. She'd positioned Sergey near the back door behind the stack of old metal and seats so that the only thing showing past the pile of the truck's fenders was his camera. The two different angles gave her an excellent view of the whole bay—except for Garret being constantly in the way.

Because she was the only one with any idea of what was going on inside the warehouse, she'd become the operation's leader. The fact that she was wholly unqualified didn't seem to matter to the others.

And she couldn't exactly argue, not without being overheard.

So she was answering tactical questions with one tap for yes and two for no.

No, the trucks weren't unloaded yet.

Yes, that really was Garret in the white *khet partug* with the brown vest.

No, not the gray *khet partug* with the white vest.

Yes, with the *kufi* hat.

Yes, it looked remarkably silly on him.

Yes, she wanted to shout. *I will bang your heads together if we get out of this alive.*

No, she didn't have a clear shot on the leader.

Because Garret, you've got to move your ass out of my way.

She looked to Sergey, but he didn't have any ideas either. They were separated by ten feet behind two different piles of junk. Then she noticed that his tail had light on it. Light from one of the trucks shining past the various debris and the engine block.

Very slowly she signaled him out of the light. The view on her wrist screen was now partially blocked by a spare tire, but there was no revealing light hitting Sergey. And the area of the warehouse that Sergey's video feed revealed allowed her to remain hidden, seeing part of the bay with one eye and the dog's angle with the other. She couldn't maintain the split vision for long, but it was enough.

The next time Garret gestured toward something on the truck he glanced back. Then he very deliberately moved aside.

She wanted to kiss him again. He'd been interfering with her picture, because he was trying to protect her dog. He'd seen Sergey's tail and been very careful to block the leader's sightline. That wasn't something a merely good man did. Only a truly wonderful one did something like that.

"I have an idea," Baxter called over the radio. His Pacific Northwest non-accent was a little flatter than Burton's. "Give me a minute."

She could feel Garret's nerves stretching thin as surely as if there was a lead in her hand but connected to Garret rather than Sergey.

In the midst of a sudden clatter from the unloaders, she risked a whispered, "More like twenty seconds."

The second truck was unloaded.

The leader, whose gun was still aimed at Garret, was looking around as if searching for something.

Then Hukam groaned behind her.

The leader twisted her way.

She rolled out into the gap between her engine block hideaway and Sergey's tire and fender pile, and shot the leader in the face over Garret's shoulder. Twice for good measure.

Garret swung free his AK-47 and between them they dropped the other unloaders. The engine roared to life. Then Garret emptied his magazine through the back window of the pickup killing the driver and another guard seated there. The truck lurched halfway out of the bay, then stalled to a stop.

The other two truck engines racketed to life.

"Let the lead driver go," Baxter called out.

There was a harsh blast from the big DShK mounted on the second truck. Stone exploded over her head as rounds from the heavy machine gun pummeled into the warehouse bay. It fired ten, half-inch rounds every second. Rock dust, machine parts, everything seemed to be flying into the air at once.

Then the big gun cut off abruptly as Jeff declared, "Got him!" Thank god for snipers.

Liza risked looking up from where she'd cowered during the fusillade.

"Feh! That's nothing, dude," Mutt transmitted just moments before all hell broke loose.

The Toyota pickup, along with its driver, the DShK, and its dead gunner lifted upward in a massive explosion. BB had planted IEDs out in the yard on just such a chance. Mutt must have triggered one that happened to be directly under the pickup.

The truck shattered. Shrapnel blew into the warehouse bay. Everything that wasn't nailed down blew in her direction.

Once again, flat on the floor, she just prayed that the recently delivered explosives didn't trigger as well.

"Whoops!" Mutt muttered when the explosion had cleared. The entire bay was brightly lit by the truck burning just outside the door. Scorch marks ran halfway down the length of both walls from the tongue of flame that had shot at them. Afghanistan was hot, but the space was now as hot as an oven and for a moment it hurt to breathe.

Garret had rolled under the partially disassembled SUV during the worst of it. Now he rolled back out and turned to look at her. He wore a boy-happy grin on a man's face. There was not even a hint of the dour, glowering boy who had haunted the high school's hallways.

The third truck engine ground gears and raced its engine as it tried to make good its escape. Garret grabbed the AK-47 from the leader's body and was scrambling toward the door.

"No!" She shouted, remembering that he didn't have a radio. "Baxter said to let it go."

Garret skidded to a halt and looked at her down the length of the bay.

She might have expected confusion, understanding, or surprise on his face. She never expected to see horror.

In that instant, not two feet behind her, she heard the unholy snarl of an enraged Malinois and the scream of a man the moment before his throat was ripped out. She spun just in time to see the steel pipe that Hukam had raised high to smash down on her head fall from nerveless fingers as he tumbled backward under Sergey's onslaught and died.

"Check it out," Baxter climbed up onto the safehouse roof and came over with his laptop.

He held it so that Garret and Liza could see it from where they were sitting side-by-side, leaning back against the roof's balustrade and watching the sunset.

"It worked."

Baxter had dropped down from the roof and ducked out into the open to attach a radio bug under the lead pickup before the firefight had begun—that's why he'd said to let it go. But knowing the Taliban would check for any stray signals, Baxter had set it to turn on after six hours, then deliver only a one-second pulse every ten minutes. Essentially undetectable unless someone was specifically listening for it. The US military had a drone up at forty-thousand feet doing just that.

"Hasn't moved in the last nine hours. Based on the imaging from the drone, I think we have our explosives supplier located."

Garret held up his hand and they traded high-fives. Baxter headed back down the ladder whistling.

Now it was just the three of them, sitting together on the roof of the safehouse—him, Liza, and Sergey with his head happily in her lap. They were just above the line of the protective barriers. High enough to see the great bowl of the Afghan sky, but not high enough to be exposed to any distant snipers on the ground.

Hukam's widow had been very forthcoming on the other caches and local bombmakers she knew around town. She'd hated her husband's fanaticism and had just wanted to live quietly and have a family. With her guidance, Afghan regular forces were going in and clearing out Hukam's former associates.

He wanted to put his arm around Liza. Hold her, pull her in tight. He'd like to—

"Is there a reason you haven't kissed me?" Liza asked the question completely matter-of-factly. She was *so* his kind of woman. Ten years of abandoned, mostly, fantasies and she kept exceeding them at every turn.

"Well, I have to admit, there are a couple."

"What? Do you want your own Kong dog toy and crunchy biscuit?"

"Not so much." He risked putting his arm around her shoulders, because if her question wasn't an invitation to enjoy himself at least that much, he didn't know what was.

Sergey's eyes followed him closely, but he didn't raise his head from her thigh.

Liza leaned into his side and he upgraded to tightening his arm into a one-armed side embrace. Still no squirm.

"First, that world-class kiss you laid on me was enough to give a man performance anxiety. Could I *ever* return that one appropriately?"

"That's crap, Garret. You were never a man to not trust himself around women. Remember I saw you in the high school halls all those years."

"Maybe I changed."

"Ehhhh!" Liza made a harsh buzzer sound of "total fail."

"Okay, caught me. Two, I know that kiss was in the heat of the moment right before a battle and—"

"Had a lot of experience with pre-battle kisses, have you?"

He couldn't help laughing. "Can't say I have."

"Should I check that with Mutt, or Jeff?"

Garret offered a fake shudder in response. "Both have beards. Ick!"

"So do you."

"But it looks good on me."

"It does," she agreed then continued before he could do more than be surprised. "So what's the real reason?"

"Got two actually. First, this mission is over for us. Out team is moving out tomorrow. Going after that explosives supplier."

"Maybe you should take me there."

"It's way into the worst country you can imagine. Through the heart of Kandahar Province into Lashkar Gah. We did three months there and it makes this place look like a Caribbean resort."

"Maybe you should take me *there* too."

Garret opened his mouth, but nothing came out. He began to wonder if he'd ever keep up with this woman.

"Bet you could use a good dog team in Kandahar."

"Bet we could," he said it slowly and carefully to give himself time to think fast. "You were a huge asset here. We'd have still been checking the first couple warehouse rows when that truck bomb was rebuilt and had crossed the border if it wasn't been for you two." He scratched Sergey's head. His hand came back unmangled, which he'd take as a good sign. In all his years he'd never seen anything like Sergey taking down a man three times his size.

"Bet we could think of something to do together at a Caribbean resort too."

The air whooshed out of him. There was no answer possible to that one. The Minnow in a bikini on a tropical beach—no Baltimore boy could be that lucky, but he could sure hope.

"What's the real reason you haven't kissed me?"

Garret smiled at her. He just couldn't help himself. As easily as he could imagine Minnow in a beach bikini, he could imagine Liza Minot in a beach wedding dress. The craziest and best part was that he could imagine himself standing right there beside her, feet planted in the sand, with a dog for a ringbearer.

"The real reason..." he trailed it out.

"Uh-huh," she looked up at him with those perfect blue eyes that he never wanted to look away from.

"I don't think Sergey would like it much."

Liza leaned down and tickled the dog's ears. "What do you think? After all, he's not quite the arrogant master sergeant we thought he was. Maybe we need to come up with a command past 'Friend'."

Sergey inspected him balefully for a long moment before heaving one of his dog sighs as if giving in to the inevitable. He shifted his position so that his back lay along her thigh, but he was now looking out at the desert. Apparently it was okay with him, but he'd rather not watch.

"Well," Liza looked up at him and Garret could feel his heart pick up the pace. "I guess Sergey doesn't really mind. And I most certainly don't."

As he leaned in to kiss her, Garret still kept one eye on the dog.

IF YOU ENJOYED THIS, YOU MIGHT
ALSO ENJOY:

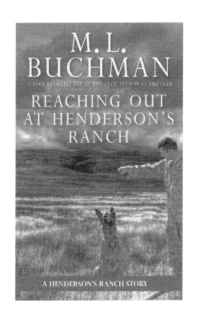

REACHING OUT AT HENDERSON'S RANCH (EXCERPT)

*H*e reached to console the frightened villager child.

Stan Corman knew it was dangerous, but he couldn't stop his hand. His left hand kept moving closer though some part of him screamed for it to withdraw, to fall by his side.

The boy, no more than five, could have been his nephew Jack. They had the same tousled dark hair, though Jack's skin was far lighter.

His hand continued to reach.

Deep inside himself, Stan cursed and fought, but his arm moved without his willing it.

No control.

Except his eyes. Though his hand remained out of his control, he could see with his eyes.

Stan could see the little boy's fear—his eyes so wide that the dark irises were almost lost in the vast field of white. He'd knelt so that they were eye to eye. Then Stan looked down and he could see his dog Lucy abruptly sit, close in front of the boy.

Lucy wasn't supposed to sit without a command unless—

Stan's hand brushed the boy's arm.

Lucy whined.

She was a military war dog and was trained to sit and be still when she smelled—

The boy disappeared in a cloud of light that slammed Stan into the void.

The scream tearing out of his throat ripped him from nightmare to darkness.

Absolute darkness...except for the afterimage of an exploding boy etched so deeply on his retina that it was all he'd been able to see when he woke in the hospital.

Now, months away, he tried to rub at his eyes as his pulse peaked somewhere past skyrocket and began a slow fall that Stan knew from experience would banish any hope of sleep for hours.

But there was no hand to rub his eyes with, only a fleshy stump remained of his left hand. His other hand was tangled in the sheets and for a long awful moment he was sure he had lost that one as well. Before he could scream again, he managed to pull it free and pressed his hand to his face.

Five.

He counted four fingers and a thumb pressed from jaw to forehead. Flesh and blood. He could feel them. Five. His right hand still remained intact.

As did the image of the exploding boy.

Stan's life had been saved because the boy's parents—or whatever total bastard had wired the kid up—had rigged the explosives too low. The alignment of explosive and Stan's life had been almost entirely shielded by Lucy's body.

The helmet had protected his head, the goggles his eyes, and except for nasty scarring on his left cheek, the rest of him had been behind armor and dog. Lucy had taken the hit and like a nuclear blast burn image, the shape of her had been imprinted on his lower face and chest in blood and bone fragments. The rest had healed: the dozen broken ribs where parts of Lucy had slammed into him, the concussion from the wall he'd been thrown into so hard that even his helmet hadn't saved him from that. They'd managed to save his left calf and knee with screws and titanium plates, but had warned him it would always be fragile. Just what every SEAL wanted to be labeled: fragile.

He lay in a cot. His pulse had slowed enough—though the rate of his breathing hadn't yet—for him to feel the hard chill of the cabin. The fire had gone out, which meant it was past three a.m.

It was a good sign. Usually the nightmare woke him by midnight in plenty of time to restoke the small cast iron woodstove for the long, sleepless dark watch. He considered waiting until dawn under the covers, but experience also had taught him to get up and build the fire now or the cabin would stay frosty until midday.

A North Carolina boy, his only experience with true cold before now had been on assignment. The Afghan winters had been brutal, but that's where Special Operations said to go—so he and Lucy went.

Lucy. Shit. They'd been together for two years in-country. She was six months dead and he still missed her every damn day.

He snapped on a flashlight, for all the good it did him. All he could see right now was the little Afghan boy etched in light. The doctors insisted that it was psychosomatic rather than retinal damage because doctors made shit like that up when they didn't know what was going on. The only part of his vision that he could use for the next hour would be in the one dark, dog-shaped patch that had been Lucy in the lower right corner of his vision.

He swung out of his bunk, tipped his head back and to the side so that he could see where he was going, and crossed to the woodstove. Grabbing the handle without a hot pad had him yelping again—not pain but a sharp, panicked sound that rang harshly in the small cabin. If he damaged his right hand he'd be beyond fucked. It was all he had left. He sucked on the slight warmth on his palm as if it was a second-degree burn, cursing the damn stove for still being hot to the touch, but not heating the cabin.

Reaching with his other hand didn't help. The paired titanium hooks of his prosthetic arm didn't care about the heat, but he hadn't pulled the rig on and all he had to wave about was his fucking stump.

Fumbling toward the woodpile, which was on the side he couldn't see, he found a small log and used it to whack the metal handle upward and swing the door open. For its duty and fine service, he chucked the log onto the few remaining embers inside.

Raising one knee, he propped a small bellows on his thigh and pinned its lower handle in place with his stump. With his remaining hand, he worked the upper handle until he coaxed a small snap of flame to life. It was bright enough to shine through the boy's afterimage. Carefully stoking the fire, he watched the flame grow as the boy faded.

The stove wasn't throwing much heat yet; all of the iron had cooled…except the goddamn handle. But he didn't move away. His bare skin rippled with goosebumps, but he remained to watch the flame.

When he'd first come to this small cabin in the Montana foothills, he'd spent many nights contemplating throwing his fake arm into the fire and then himself. At first he only resisted because he knew he'd piss off the ranch owner, and you didn't piss off a man like Mac Henderson or his son Mark.

Mac was a former SEAL—except he'd done his twenty years and retired. Being a SEAL, it was an easy bet that Mac would have followed Stan straight into hell and dragged him back to whup him good for throwing away the gift of life.

Gift of life, my ass.

It was early April. Back in North Carolina, the Sweet William would be blooming right now. The cherry blossoms would have already had their spring and the young cottonwood leaves would be unfolding to seek the sun.

Instead, he was squatting in front of a cold fire in a ramshackle cabin on the edge of the Montana wilderness surrounded by snow. It wasn't the life he'd pictured. But the life he'd pictured had thrown him out on his ass. When he'd gone home, his mother had burst into tears every time she looked at him. His fiancé hadn't even bothered to Dear Stan him. True love hadn't even lasted out the month for the half-man he'd become to make it out of the hospital. His sister had forced Stan's brother-in-law to offer him a pity-job at the bank, as if Stan would be forever helpless. Besides, there was no way he could ever survive working indoors. And young nephew Jack had taken one look at his steel hooks and run away screaming in terror—as terrified as the little boy in the Afghan village.

Then one day he'd gotten a call from his former CO to come over to Fort Bragg. It was the last place in the world for a one-armed former SEAL to be, but saying no to Lieutenant Commander Luke Altman wasn't something a man did.

Altman had met him at the gate, which was a real favor. It saved him having to kill every damn grunt who stared at the hooks sticking out of his shirt sleeve and gave him that you-ain't-a-soldier-no-more look.

"Got someone I want you to meet."

"I don't need another goddamn therapist or perky wounded warrior volunteer to tell me how to live with myself."

Altman had merely looked over at him in that long, quiet

way he had and Stan shut up. Altman took him to the SWCS dining hall. It was strange to be back on the JFK Special Warfare Center and School grounds and not be ragged from their typically brutal training scenarios. He hadn't let himself go after getting released, but he hadn't done a decent workout either—not with one fucking hand. The month on his back had cost him a lot of muscle and the PT hadn't really put it back on—weird to trade the military's Physical Training acronym (or Puking Torture depending on who was leading the drill) in for medical's Physical Therapy, which told him just how civilian he'd become.

They grabbed trays and went down the line. Stan had learned enough about working his hooks to not need any help. Actually, having been left-handed before the injury, he was almost better with the hooks than with his clumsy right hand. It had become almost natural that when he extended his arm, or flexed his opposite shoulder, the two hooks separated and when he withdrew or relaxed they clamped together tight. Stan used them to load up on he didn't care what and went to sit with another pair of civilians—the ex-military kind by the look of them.

"Stan Corman. This is Mark Henderson and Emily Beale. Former Night Stalkers who founded the 5D."

Okay, that got Stan's attention. The Night Stalkers Special Operations Aviation Regiment specialized in helicopter transport for soldiers like him—like he'd been. He'd flown with SOAR plenty of times, but never with the 5D. They were practically legendary and were always with the very top teams, Delta and DEVGRU. He hadn't known one was a woman, but nothing surprised him about the 5D. If these were the founders… But shit! They were still intact. What was their goddamn excuse?

"They," Altman was still yammering, "have a place that they're going to tell you about. His dad runs the ranch and

Mac trained me back in the day. Stan, you're going to shut up and listen."

Shutting up and listening had never been his top skill, but not arguing with his CO—former or otherwise—had been too ingrained, especially when it was SEAL Commander Luke Altman.

And that meeting had led to him squatting naked in front of a woodstove at the far corner of Henderson's Ranch in snowy April.

The dawn had happened at some point while he watched and fed the fire. The purging by flame no longer beckoned to him, but its warmth didn't comfort him either.

He was never going to fit back in. His dog was gone. Two of his team also had been close enough that they'd gone home in a box. The other two had gone down in a hail of crossfire that filled two more boxes. Left for dead; he'd been the "lucky one."

The lucky one.

No team. No unit. No longer a soldier. He'd lost fiancé, family, and town.

There was no one who wanted him. No place he belonged. The dead end was staring him in the face and there was no reverse gear out of it. His future was bricked in as surely as the sides of the glowing iron box filled with ashes and fire. Who would give a shit if the flames did consume him? Easy answer. The future held noth—

A knock sounded on the cabin door. The sudden sound where there shouldn't be any sent him diving for cover behind the woodpile. All it earned him was a couple of splinters before he recovered and remembered where he was.

Furious with himself for sliding back into the black hole of panic and depression, he strode to the door and reached for it with his stump, then yanked it open with his right hand and a snarl.

Ama Henderson stood there with her horse tethered to the porch rail behind her. Mac's wife was a tall, magnificent woman. Her skin was still dark and smooth, but her hair had turned that dark steel-gray that was so unique to her Cherokee heritage.

"May I come in?"

It was a several-hour ride from the main house to the cabin that they'd given him; a damned cold one. The sun… he'd lost time again. It was a couple of hours above the snowy horizon in the crystal blue that was a Montana winter sky.

He held the door wider and the chill wind wrapped around him and reminded him that he was naked.

"Shit! Excuse me." He left Ama to close the door as he dragged on some clothes as well as he could. They were icy cold because he'd dropped them on the floor last night rather than on the chair by the stove. Without his arm on, it proved impossible to pull on underwear and pants.

Hating it, he stood there naked and dragged on a t-shirt first. He couldn't stand people seeing him put on his arm—not even the docs who'd fit it and trained him—but he had no choice. He found the thin cotton sock and pulled it up over his stump, careful to smooth out any wrinkles despite his haste. Then he unsnarled the harness, slipped his stump through one loop and into the socket of the prosthesis. With a practiced lean, he managed to get his good arm through the harness' other loop on his first try, thank god, and shrug it on. Now able to control the spring action of the paired hooks, he was able to drag on underwear, socks, and pants. A heavy jacket against the still cool cabin—he hadn't closed the woodstove's door and damped the fire to get good heat from it—and then he jammed his feet into his boots, though he'd be damned if he'd demonstrate for anyone how clumsy he still was at lacing them.

When he turned back, Ama was sitting at the small table looking down into a bundle she'd been carrying. Kind enough to offer him privacy while he struggled.

"Sorry, Ama. Can I offer you some coffee?"

He kicked the woodstove door shut, almost losing one of his unlaced boots into the fire in the process.

"No. I have come to offer *you* something."

As he'd learned was typical with her, she didn't say much but when she did, there was no point in either interrupting or attempting to hurry her to the point. So, he sat in the other chair and waited.

She looked at him with her intensely dark eyes. "You have decided that you don't want to stay at the main compound. I can respect that. There are times that a man must face his future alone. But there is also a time for that to end. My husband would leave you until spring to stew in your own thoughts. By then the pot will boil over. I do not choose to leave you so long."

He readied his protests that he wasn't fit to be neighbor to man or beast. His screams alone as he rose from each night's dreams were proof enough of that. What if they never ended? What would he do then?

Apparently done with what she had to say, she stood and headed for the door leaving her bundle on the table.

"Ama. I—" he called after her, but the bundle on the table moved. In the moment of his distraction, she was gone out the door. He knew that even if he rushed after her, she would somehow be gone, departing as quietly across the snow as she'd arrived.

The bundle moved again.

Then a nose stuck out the top.

It sniffed the air once, twice, then the rest of the head emerged and the puppy turned to look at him. Its dark face wore the goofy grin that could only be a Malinois—the same breed as almost every war dog. The same breed as Lucy.

Stan stared at it in horror, not even able to tear his eyes away to look at the door where Ama Henderson had left him.

A dog.

He couldn't even care for himself; how was he supposed to care for a dog?

The puppy yipped at him and he flinched.

It wasn't fair. He would end up killing it just as his one mistake had killed every other good thing around him.

ABOUT THE AUTHOR

M.L. Buchman started the first of, what is now over 50 novels and as many short stories, while flying from South Korea to ride his bicycle across the Australian Outback. Part of a solo around the world trip that ultimately launched his writing career.

All three of his military romantic suspense series—The Night Stalkers, Firehawks, and Delta Force—have had a title named "Top 10 Romance of the Year" by the American Library Association's *Booklist.* NPR and Barnes & Noble have named other titles "Top 5 Romance of the Year." In 2016 he was a finalist for Romance Writers of America prestigious RITA award. He also writes: contemporary romance, thrillers, and fantasy.

Past lives include: years as a project manager, rebuilding and single-handing a fifty-foot sailboat, both flying and jumping out of airplanes, and he has designed and built two houses. He is now making his living as a full-time writer on the Oregon Coast with his beloved wife and is constantly amazed at what you can do with a degree in Geophysics. You may keep up with his writing and receive a free starter e-library by subscribing to his newsletter at: www.mlbuchman.com

Join the conversation:
www.mlbuchman.com

Other works by M. L. Buchman:

SIGN UP FOR M. L. BUCHMAN'S
NEWSLETTER TODAY

and receive:
Release News
Free Short Stories
a Free Starter Library

Do it today. Do it now.
www.mlbuchman.com/newsletter

Printed in Great Britain
by Amazon